TWIST ◆ PLOT™

HORRORS
—OF THE—
HAUNTED MUSEUM

R.L. STINE

Interior illustrations by David G. Klein

SCHOLASTIC INC.
New York Toronto London Auckland Sydney

No part of this publication may be reproduced in whole or in part, or stored in a retrieval system, or transmitted in any form or by any means, electronic, mechanical, photocopying, recording, or otherwise, without written permission of the publisher. For information regarding permission, write to Scholastic Inc., 555 Broadway, New York, NY 10012.

ISBN 0-590-48556-3

Text copyright © 1983 by Robert Stine. Illustrations copyright © 1994 by Scholastic Inc. All rights reserved. Published by Scholastic Inc. APPLE PAPERBACKS and TWISTAPLOT are registered trademarks of Scholastic Inc.

12 11 10 9 8 7 6 5 4 3 2 1   10   4 5 6 7 8 9/9

Printed in the U.S.A.   40

BEWARE!!!
DO NOT READ THIS BOOK FROM BEGINNING TO END!

Y**ou** are about to spend a long and frightening night in the City Historical Museum. Everyone knows that this creepy old place is rumored to be haunted—haunted by mummies, by ghouls, and by ghostly spirits that prowl its dark rooms when the sun goes down.

By spending a night in this museum of mystery, you hope to find out whether the rumors are true. Unfortunately, you just may find out *more than you wish to know!*

As you make your way through the museum's darkened rooms, you will make your own decisions. You will choose your own paths by following the instructions at the bottom of each page.

If you make the right moves, you will have many adventures to tell your friends about the next morning. If you make the wrong moves, you will soon discover why this book is called *HORRORS of the Haunted Museum!*

Now, *pay your admission*, and *enter* the museum on *PAGE 2.*

"You're not serious about spending the night in this place . . . are you?" your friend Mike asks.

"Of *course* I'm serious," you reply, leaning against a totem pole in the far corner of the American Indian Room. "Kelly and Derek both dared us, and we accepted. We can't chicken out now."

Mike rests his elbows on top of a glass case that contains an authentic model of an Indian pueblo. "But you don't believe all that garbage about this museum being haunted—about the mummy coming to life every night. And neither do I. So what's the point?" he asks.

"The point is, they dared us," you say.

A bell rings, the signal that the museum is closing. A museum guard pokes his head into the American Indian Room, but he doesn't see you or Mike.

"The point is, I don't care. I'm going home," Mike says.

"Maybe you're a little scared, after all," you suggest. Mike waves a fist at you in pretend anger.

The bell rings again. You hear the footsteps on the marble floor of the last people leaving the museum. The two of you continue to argue. Your mind is made up—you're spending the night in the museum.

Will you be able to convince Mike to stay with you? Turn to PAGE 12.

4

"Follow me," you say boldly to the pirates, making a broad gesture with your arm. You swagger as you lead them into the woods, hoping to convince them you know where you're going.

"It's good ye decided to c'operate," the pirate with the dagger says, coming up and putting a hot, damp arm around your shoulder. "That'll make Captain Johnny right pleased. An' when the captain is pleased, it goes better for the rest of us swabs—right, men?"

The pirates agree heartily.

They continue to follow you deeper and deeper into the woods. Mike keeps giving you questioning looks, but you ignore him and keep walking.

"Maybe ye be needin' a map," the pirate says to you after you've been leading them around in circles for close to an hour. "Or maybe ye been havin' a little fun with us?"

"We're almost there," you say quietly.

"Don't be temptin' Dickie Dagger now," the pirate threatens. "He's got a quick temper—and he's mean."

"You must be nuts!" Mike whispers. "They're going to *kill* us when they see you're leading us around in circles."

Go on to *PAGE* 5.

"Look at them," you reply. "They're exhausted. They're worn out. I'll get them even more tired. Then we'll split."

You keep them walking around in circles for another half hour. Then you stop and point to a tall tree. "Dig three paces to the left of that tree," you say dramatically.

The pirates, who have been dragging their shovels along with them during your long walk, begin to dig.

And dig.

And dig.

Soon they are four feet down, digging a deeper and deeper hole.

"Okay—let's get outta here!" Mike whispers.

"Where would we go?" you ask. "This seems to be a small island. If we run away, they'll just catch up to us. I think we have to fight them. Look—I can grab the dagger away from that pirate easy. If we fight them, we can force them to take us off this island on their boat."

To run—or to fight—that's the choice you have to make now while the pirates are busily digging.

If you choose to run, turn to PAGE 26.
If you choose to fight, turn to PAGE 38.

6

The two of you turn and run as fast as you can into the mummy room. The room is dark. Two nightlights against the far wall give off a faint orange glow.

Did the slow footsteps go the other way?

Scrape. Scrape.

No!

Someone, something still pursues you.

You hear the scraping of a heavy foot dragging across the marble floor. Then a footstep. Then the dragging foot again.

Scrape. Step. Scrape.

You try to say something to Mike. You're so scared that your mouth opens but no sounds come out.

In the darkness you can see that he is as frightened as you are.

Scrape. Step. Scrape.

The footsteps stop. Silence. All you can hear now is the pounding of your heart, the ticking of your watch.

Scrape. Step. Scrape.

They start again. Closer. So close you feel as if you could reach out and grab whatever is walking toward you in the dark, cold room.

"The mummy!" you finally manage to whisper to Mike. "It must be the mummy! It sounds like a mummy!"

"You mean . . ." Mike says, "the rumors are true?!?"

Go on to PAGE 7.

Scrape. Step.

"Quick—into the pyramid!" you whisper, pulling at Mike's sleeve. "Whatever it is won't look for us in there!"

You both look at the giant, reconstructed pyramid across the room from you.

"No!" Mike cries. "We'll be trapped in there. Who knows what's *in* there? They moved it stone by stone from Egypt!"

"Who knows what's out here?!" you cry.

Scrape. Step. *Scrape.*

You'd better decide fast. Should you run into the pyramid to hide? Or should you stay and face whoever is approaching?

If you choose the pyramid, turn to PAGE 20.

If you choose not to move from your hiding place, turn to PAGE 10.

"Don't stand there bejabberin' if'n ye know what's best for ye," the pirate captain calls.

You are so stunned that this mannequin has come to life that you follow the pirate's instructions. You and Mike walk up the gangplank of the model ship, and before you know it, you are standing on the deck, facing what seems to be a living eighteenth-century pirate!

"Allow me to introduce meself to ye," the captain says with a small bow. "I be Captain Johnny Poison, sailing these many years under the proud flag of the Jolly Roger."

"Uh . . . how do you do . . ." you manage to blurt out.

"Not well, me hearty. Not well," he replies, scratching his stubble of a beard. "I be landlocked here. Can't get a wind to fill me sails. A windless sky means a lonely life for Captain Johnny."

"Gosh, that's too bad," you say. You stare at this character from two centuries ago and ask yourself, *Can this really be happening?*

"There's nothing we can do to help," Mike says.

"I'd be thinkin' twice before ye utter those words, lad," the pirate says, his face squinting into an evil frown. He pulls out his broadsword and holds it up to your throat. "Ye'll help me—or face me blade!"

Go on to PAGE 9.

Without thinking, you reach your hand over to the captain's table and pick up another sword that is lying there. You take a step back and raise the sword to fight.

"Wait!" Mike cries. "Don't fight! We'll help you, Captain Johnny. We'll do something!"

Has Mike lost his mind? What can you possibly do to help this pirate?

You must decide what to do—fight him so that you can get off this mysterious ship, or agree to help him and then pray that you can think of something.

If you choose to fight, turn to PAGE 18.
If you agree to help him, turn to PAGE 24.

Scrape. Scrape.

"Who's there?" you suddenly yell out.

Why did you do that?

"Shut up!" Mike whispers. "Are you nuts?"

"Who's there?" you call again.

There is no answer.

Scrape. Scrape.

"We've got to get out of here!" you tell Mike, shaking all over.

"Yes—but not into the pyramid," he insists.

"Okay, okay. Let's head for that door over there."

"What room does it lead to?"

"How should I know?" you scream. "I'm not a tour guide! All I know is it leads *out* of here!"

"No," Mike says, "I'm not going unless I know where I'm going."

"You'd rather face whatever it is that's dragging its way to us?" you cry. "Come on, Mike. Let's get going!"

Stay or go through the door into an unknown room? That's your choice now.

_____

If you pick the unknown room, turn to PAGE 30.

If once again you choose to stay where you are, turn to PAGE 36.

"It's a dumb idea. We'll only get in trouble," Mike says, starting to walk toward the exit. "What about our parents?"

"We took care of that," you remind him. "You said you were staying over at my house, and I said I was staying over at your house."

Another museum guard passes by, but he doesn't see the two of you in the far corner. Outside the room's only window, you see that the sun has almost set. The museum grows silent. The silence is complete.

"I'm sorry," Mike says, "but I just don't want to do this. I'm not chicken or anything. I just want to go home and have supper. See ya."

He walks quickly toward the main hall and the exit. You start to go after him, but you change your mind.

Okay. Fine, you tell yourself. *I'll stay here without him.*

You listen to his footsteps clicking on the cold floors, fading into the distance. The lights in the room dim. The air conditioner shuts off.

You stand and wait for your eyes to adjust to the darkness. A few minutes go by.

Go on to PAGE 13.

What a story this will be to tell! Just about everyone you know has talked about spending the night in this creepy place—but you *are actually doing it!*

Hey . . . wait a minute! What are those footsteps?

They're getting louder. They're definitely coming your way.

Slow, s-l-o-w footsteps.

Who could be walking so slowly, so quietly?

Should you turn and run? Or should you wait to see who approaches?

If you choose to run, turn to PAGE 19.

If you choose to see who is coming, turn to PAGE 22.

The narrow corridors lead to wider rooms. The rooms lead to narrow, curving corridors. The rooms are all empty except for the spiders that have made the pyramid their home, filling every corner with thick webs.

"Have we been in this room before?" Mike asks.

"I can't tell," you admit. "They all look alike."

"How long have we been walking? It seems like hours and hours," Mike says, his voice a lot higher than usual.

"I don't think it's been that long," you say, struggling to control your voice. "We've got to stay calm, Mike. We can't panic. There's got to be a way out of this creepy place. The museum wouldn't put up a pyramid without at least a couple of exits—right?"

Mike doesn't answer.

"I know," you say, struggling to sound cheerful. "Let's just turn around and go back the way we came in."

"Which way is that?" Mike asks gloomily.

He's right. You don't remember which way you came in. You've made so many twists and turns in these dark halls that you've lost all sense of direction. "It's this way, I'm pretty sure," you say, even though you're not pretty sure.

Go on to PAGE 15.

"Maybe we should just wait here for someone to find us," Mike suggests.

"But, Mike, no one knows we're here, remember?" you say. "Come on, we've got to look on the bright side. At least we lost the mummy that was chasing us."

"Maybe," Mike mutters.

You walk a little farther, your flashlights moving quickly up and down over the gray, cracked walls. Suddenly you enter a large chamber. At the far end of it, you can make out two doors.

One door leads into a brightly lit chamber. A sign hangs over the doorway. Someone has translated the hieroglyphics. It reads: CURSED BE THOSE WHO DARE TO ENTER THIS CHAMBER OF TREASURE.

The other door seems to lead into more darkness.

"I'm not going into a room with a curse on it," Mike says. "I don't care *how* bright and cheerful it is in there!"

"But the other room is as dark and empty as all the others we've been through," you argue. "Maybe this room is bright because it leads out of the pyramid."

Which doorway do you choose to go through?

If you choose the doorway with the curse above it, turn to PAGE 32.

If you choose the other doorway, turn to PAGE 46.

"These owls are three times as big as normal owls!" you cry. "And they look three times as mean!"

"How can we fight them?" Mike asks, looking around the room.

You look desperately around the room for some kind of weapon. But there are only decorations and treasure chests.

The owls swoop right by your faces, screeching at the top of their lungs, their eyes narrow slits of evil, their mouths pulled back tightly in attack grins.

You dodge away from one that swoops at you, then duck behind a chest as two more plunge downward.

"We can't fight them!" Mike cries. "And we can't keep ducking them forever!"

But the attack stops as suddenly as it began.

The owls stop their furious flapping. They glide now up to the top of the wall where the molding forms a ledge. They glide up to the ledge, their eyes closing, and land softly.

"Look—that's where they nest," you whisper to Mike.

The two of you stare in disbelief.

"They—they're going to sleep!" you cry.

The owls seem to puff up as they lower their feathered heads into their bodies, close their eyes—and sleep.

Go on to PAGE 17.

"I don't believe it! I just don't believe it!" Mike cries.

"I do," you say, with a big smile. "It's so bright in here, Mike. It's as bright as day-light."

"Yeah. So what?"

"Owls sleep in daylight. They're night creatures—remember?"

"Right. Night creatures. What a lucky break! Now if we could only get out of here."

"*With* the treasure!" you add.

Can you get out—with the treasure? Turn to PAGE 82.

You raise the sword and swing it with all your strength. It goes right through the pirate captain!

You swing again. The sword goes right through him as if he isn't there!

"Y-you're nothing but a ghost!" you scream.

Captain Johnny drops his sword. He lowers his eyes, as if embarrassed, and shrugs his shoulders sadly. You put down your sword, too. You actually find yourself feeling sorry for the poor guy.

Then you see something out of the corner of your eye. "I think I can help you, Captain," you say. You turn and walk down the gangplank. Mike follows right behind you.

You walk over to a table on the other side of the museum room. There's a large electric fan on the table. "This should help, Captain Johnny!" you yell across the room.

You turn on the fan and watch as the pirate ship's sails fill with wind.

"Ah, a fine wind! Thank ye kindly!" Captain Johnny says, with a big grin. He gives you a wave as the ship sails off out of sight.

"That didn't really happen . . . did it??" Mike asks.

You don't know what to say. The two of you are standing in an absolutely empty room!

THE END

The slow, s-l-o-w footsteps are coming nearer.

Your heart is pounding in your chest.

Whoever it is has entered the American Indian Room. Whoever it is must know that someone is in the room!

You turn to run, and—

Whaaaaam!

You run headfirst into a glass display case.

Ouch! You never knew glass was so hard!

You sit down until you stop seeing stars. It is too late to run now.

You have no choice but to face whoever—or whatever—is pursuing you!

Turn to PAGE 22.

Scrape. Step.

The footsteps approach, slow but steady, one foot stepping with a loud click on the marble floor, the other foot dragging slowly forward with a dry, scraping sound.

"I'm not hanging around to find out what that is!" you whisper to Mike.

You turn and run into the open pyramid.

You don't even look back to see if Mike is following you. But the sounds of running feet and hard breathing tell you that he is right behind you.

It is dark in the pyramid, but the long, narrow corridor you find yourself running through is straight. You are running to escape whatever is pursuing you, and you don't think about what lies ahead in this replica of an ancient Egyptian burial tomb.

"Wait! Stop a minute!" you cry to Mike, your voice echoing again and again through the cavernous structure. You both stop and listen. Are you being followed?

No.

No footsteps.

Go on to PAGE 21.

"We've lost him!" you cry happily.

Mike struggles to catch his breath. "Great," he says, his voice still a whisper. "But *now* where are we?"

The corridor makes a right turn and then a left turn. "There has to be an exit around here somewhere," you say. "If only we could see where—"

And then you burst out laughing. You realize you've both forgotten about something.

"Our flashlights!" you say, reaching into your pack. "We forgot we brought flashlights! I don't believe it!"

With your flashlights on, you can see where you are going. You can see the gray, rotting walls, see the damp cracks in the crumbling stone floor, see the spiderwebs hanging from the ceilings.

The one thing you cannot see is a way out.

"Mike," you say, your voice shaking, "I think we're really lost."

Can you find your way out of the ancient pyramid? Turn to PAGE 14 to find out.

You've never known true terror before—but you're pretty sure that's what you're feeling now!

Your arms and legs are shaking so badly you're not sure you can get them to move. The footsteps come closer . . . closer.

Who is it? It can't be the night watchman. He'd be carrying a flashlight.

Perhaps the stories about this old museum are true! Perhaps the mummy really does walk the floors at night!

Perhaps . . .

"Hi, it's me," Mike says. "I'm back. The door was already locked. I couldn't get out. I had a hard time finding you in the dark. I had to walk really slow so I wouldn't bump into anything. Hey, are you all right?"

"Fine," you say. "I'm fine." You wait a few seconds for your heart to stop pounding. "Guess we're in this thing together now, just the two of us," you say finally.

"Uh-oh," Mike says, suddenly grabbing your arm. "I think it's the three of us!"

Sure enough, there are new footsteps clicking on the marble floor. These footsteps are approaching quickly.

"Stay calm, stay calm," you whisper to Mike. "Stay calm."

"Stop repeating yourself," Mike whispers. "Have you gone nuts or something?"

Go on to PAGE 23.

"This is no time for a discussion," you whisper. "We've got to get outta here!"

"Good thinking," Mike whispers.

The footsteps are in the same room as you. Has someone heard the two of you? Or is someone making his ghostly rounds in his nightly search for human victims?

Staying close together so that you can see each other, you and Mike run into the back hallway. Two rooms stand in front of you. To escape the approaching footsteps, you must duck into the Egyptian Mummy Room—or the Caribbean Pirates Room.

Quick—make your choice.

If you choose the mummy room, turn to PAGE 6.

If you choose the pirates room, turn to PAGE 34.

"Wait a second! We can help you," you say, putting down the sword. "Sure, we can. Right, Mike?"

"Right," Mike says, without hesitating.

"Okay, I'll spare ye," Captain Johnny says. "Pity a poor old sea dog who has to call on the likes o' you two for help."

"Uh . . . let's see now . . ." you say, looking around the ship, stalling for time. "Let's have a look down below."

You try to look at the below cabins, but there aren't any. This is only a model ship, after all. It was built only for show; it isn't really a complete, seaworthy ship.

As you look around, you quickly realize that Captain Johnny is all alone, the only crewman on this vessel. "Doesn't the poor guy realize he's in a museum?" Mike asks.

The two of you don't know *what* you can do to help the ghostly captain—*and he is beginning to realize it!*

"Captain Johnny's gonna have to feed ye to the sharks, ya swabs!" he cries angrily. "Which one o' ye is volunteerin' to walk the plank first?"

Walk the plank?? What can you do now? Keep stalling? Or walk the plank and figure you'll end up back on the museum floor, where you can run for it?

If you choose to stall, turn to PAGE 37.

If you choose to walk the plank, turn to PAGE 48.

You drop the spear and turn to run.

"Hey—the door's closed!" you yell.

"Who closed it?" Mike cries. "I know I didn't!"

You run up to the door and try to open it.

It won't budge.

You struggle to turn the handle. You push with all your strength.

You can't open it.

You have no choice but to face the attacking ancient skeletons.

Pick up your spears and turn to PAGE 44.

"Okay—let's go!" you yell.

You and Mike don't hesitate for a second. You take off, running through the woods at breakneck speed—until you run right into Captain Johnny Poison and eight of his men!

"Ye two wouldn't be desertin' me for a second time, would ye?" Captain Johnny yells, squinting up his face into an evil frown.

The pirates quickly surround you and drag you back to the hole which their cohorts have dug. Captain Johnny orders that shovels be handed to you and Mike.

"Dig away, me hearties—and if ye find nothin' but dirt in that hole, ye'll spend eternity down there! Haw haw!" He pokes you with the tip of his sword blade. "Now, dig!"

You and Mike begin to dig. The dirt flies as you go deeper into the soft earth. "We're doomed, doomed," Mike mutters, digging with slow, machinelike motions.

Suddenly your shovel hits something hard. You quickly scrape the dirt away. It's something dark and hard—like a treasure chest!

"Treasure!" you cry in amazement. "There's—there's really treasure down there!"

Go on to PAGE 27.

Mike tosses his shovel up in the air jubilantly. "We're saved! We're saved!" he cries.

A broad smile bursts across your face. You cannot contain your happiness. "Yippeeee!"

You brush away a little more dirt from the heavy object you are uncovering.

"Oh. Wait a minute," you say. "Forget everything. It's just a big rock."

Forget everything is right. You might as well stop digging. You are already in over your heads, if you dig our meaning.

Hope you uncover a better ending to your next adventure in the Haunted Museum.

THE END

Battling the waves, you swim to the island, cannonballs whizzing over your heads. You drag yourselves onto the beach and struggle to catch your breath.

"We been waitin' fer ye!" a gruff voice calls from behind you. Four pirates step out from behind the low, bent trees at the edge of the sand.

"Wha . . . ??" you manage to blurt out, your heart still pounding from your swim.

"Don't dawdle with me, shark meat," one pirate says, with a nasty frown. He pulls a long dagger out of its scabbard and gestures toward you with it. "Take us to where your treasure is buried. You know how restless Dickie Dagger can get, if you catch my meaning."

"Uh . . . let's take him to where the treasure is buried," Mike whispers to you, trembling.

"What—are you crazy?" you whisper back. "What treasure? Look—they don't have guns. Let's just run! Okay, Mike?"

Mike stands there, staring straight ahead at the pirate with the dagger.

"We be growin' impatient with ye," the pirate says. "It's best we be on our way to findin' that chest o' yours. Captain Johnny would be sore disappointed if ye both happened to meet with an unfortunate accident here. Haw haw!"

Go on to PAGE 29.

"Come on, let's take them to the treasure," Mike whispers. "We'll lead them into the woods. It'll be easier to get away once we're there. We don't stand a chance on this open beach."

"I'm not so sure," you argue. "Maybe we should run away now."

You must decide.

If you think it best to pretend to lead them to the treasure and then try to lose them in the woods, turn to PAGE 4.

If you'd rather start running now, turn to PAGE 40.

"Let's go!" you scream. You grab Mike's sleeve and pull him toward the door. The two of you run at top speed.

Scrape. Step.

The footsteps are right behind you. You can almost feel the hot mummy breath on your back!

You run through the doorway into another dark room. You stop. You look around, trying to figure out where you are, and as your eyes get used to the darkness, you realize you are looking at . . .

BONES!

Gigantic skeletons.

"It's the fossils room," you say.

"What about the footsteps? Is he following us in here?" Mike says, breathing hard and fast.

The two of you stop and listen. "Stop breathing so hard!" you yell at Mike.

"It isn't me—it's *you*!" he cries.

You both start to laugh. The footsteps are not following you.

"Whatever it was, we lost him," you say. "This is turning out to be an exciting night."

"Too exciting," Mike says. "I don't know why I let you talk me into—"

Craaaaaack!

Go on to PAGE 31.

"What was that??" you cry.

"I don't know," Mike says. "I'm pretending I didn't hear anything."

Creak. Creak. Craaack.

The two of you look quickly around the dark cavern of a room to see if anything is moving. All is still. The giant skeletons of long-dead animals stand silent.

Creak. Creak.

Suddenly a deafening roar blasts across the room and echoes off the high walls. It is followed by another roar and then a ferocious growl.

Two giant skeletons move toward you. The floor seems to rumble and shake. The ancient bones creak as they move, but the two creatures move fast. They seem to be bears, but five times the size of today's bears. They keep coming, lowering their giant jaws, roaring, clattering, rumbling—practically on top of you.

"Here, Mike—grab that spear!" you yell, picking up an ancient spear to use as a weapon against the invading skeletons.

"Are you crazy?" Mike cries. "Let's run back to the mummy room!"

You must decide—stay and fight, or go back to face whatever creature awaits in the mummy room.

If you choose to stay, turn to PAGE 44.

If you choose to return to the mummy room, turn to PAGE 25.

"Those ancient Egyptian curses only work in bad old horror movies with Boris Karloff," you tell Mike. "Don't worry about a stupid curse."

"What do you know about ancient curses?" Mike asks, backing away. "They wouldn't put curses up above the doorway if they didn't work."

"Look, Mike, it also says it's a treasure room," you say, shining your flashlight across the words on the sign. "You wouldn't mind finding some ancient treasure and becoming rich, would you?"

"I just want to get out of here in one piece," Mike insists. "I don't want a curse on my head for the rest of my life. I just want *out!*"

"Come on—calm down." You put a hand on his shoulder. "Follow me. I'm pretty sure this will lead us out of here."

Still holding onto Mike's shoulder, you walk under the curse sign and through the doorway into the brightly lit chamber.

It takes a while for your eyes to adjust. But when they do, you find yourself in a richly decorated room with bright tapestries on the walls and thick, colorful carpeting. Then you see several large, hand-carved chests against the walls.

"Wow!" you cry. "Imagine! This incredible room hidden deep in this pyramid. And look. Look at the treasure chests!"

Go on to PAGE 33.

You rush forward and open one of the chests. It's filled to the top with jewelry and ancient gold coins.

"Mike—come here! Look! It really is treasure! Unbelievable!" you cry. Your eyes are dazzled by the glittering gold and jewels under your hands. "Mike, we're rich!"

"We've got to get out of here first," Mike says, not sharing your enthusiasm.

"Hey, no problem—" you start to say, but you stop because you hear something.

Flapping wings.

The sound of dozens of flapping wings.

Suddenly, into the treasure chamber fly dozens of giant owls, fierce expressions on their faces—long-beaked owls with their talons raised, ready to attack.

"Quick—run!" Mike yells.

"No!" You try to stop him. "If we run, we'll get even more lost—and we'll lose the treasure! '

Do you choose to run away from these attacking owls—or stay and try to fight them off?

If you choose to run, turn to PAGE 60.
If you choose to stay and fight, turn to PAGE 16.

You run through the doorway into the Caribbean Pirates Room. In the dim light you can make out the life-sized pirate ship that you've seen many times before. Standing in the bow of the ship is a mannequin of a pirate captain, wearing a long-handled saber at his waist and a black eye patch over one eye.

"I don't hear the footsteps anymore," you say to Mike as you look around this familiar museum room. "I think we lost him, whoever it was."

"Hey, look at that pirate captain," Mike says, a little louder than you'd wish. "They fixed him up. Remember? He was all beat up and his clothes were torn the last time we were here."

"Come aboard, maties," a gravelly voice says suddenly. You look up to see the pirate captain beckoning down to you from his place in the ship. "Come aboard sprightly now. Old Johnny Poison's been expectin' ye!"

You don't know what to do!

Do you take your chances aboard the pirate ship with Captain Johnny Poison? Or do you turn down his invitation and try to run away from this mannequin-come-to-life?

If you choose to go aboard the ship, turn to PAGE 8.

If you choose to run, turn to PAGE 42.

Scrape. Step. Scrape.

"Okay, okay!" you scream, as the footsteps get even closer. "We're here! We're right here! Show yourself!" Your voice sounds strange to you, filled with terror.

"There's no need to shout," a man's voice cries out. "Give an old man's ears a break, willya?"

Scrape. Step.

"I'm comin' as fast as I can. It's not easy to get around with this cast on my leg."

It's the night watchman.

"I thought I heard someone in here," he says, leaning on a mummy case to catch his breath. "Just when I was looking forward to a peaceful, relaxin' evening. I gotta stay off this broken foot, ya know."

You and Mike are still speechless. He leads you to his watch post.

"Every month or so some kids just like you decide to spend the night to see if there really are ghosts in this museum. Well, I'm ready for you. Look." He leads you to two cots he has set up. "Go ahead. Spend the night. Then you can tell everyone tomorrow how brave you were."

"Sleep on a cot. Wow! What a thrill!" Mike says grumpily.

"That's okay with me," you say. "As far as I'm concerned, this night has already been exciting enough!"

THE END

"Wait a minute, Captain. We've just begun to ... uh ... let's not be hasty ... uh ..." You look around desperately, trying to think of something, *anything!*

Then, suddenly, you get an idea.

"Follow me," you tell the captain, who continues to eye you suspiciously. You lead him and Mike down the gangplank and across the floor of the museum room—into the next room!

"You're a genius!" Mike cries, seeing what's in the next room.

"What is this—some kinda black magic?" Captain Johnny cries, drawing his sword and taking a step back.

"It's called a steamship," you tell him. "Climb aboard. Give it a try."

A few moments later, the old pirate is on board the steamship. The old engine chokes and sputters and then roars. The steamship sails out of sight.

You and Mike walk back to the Caribbean Pirates Room. "We were dreaming, right?" Mike asks, shaking his head. "That was some kinda weird optical illusion or something, right?"

"Yes, of course," you say. "Look—the pirate ship is standing here as it always has."

"Yeah," says Mike, "but where is Captain Johnny?"

The model ship is now completely empty!

THE END

"We can't dig much longer. We haven't strength in our bones," one of the pirates complains.

Those are words you're happy to hear. You reach down and pull the dagger away from the pirate carrying it. "Keep digging," you yell, "or feel the blade!" You surprise yourself with your own courage.

"Nice try, swabs," a pirate cries, leaping up from the hole, "but my sword will put an end to any plans ye might be harboring."

"Hey—I thought they were exhausted!" Mike cries in alarm.

"Stop in the name of the King!" a powerful voice cries out. You turn to see a crew of British naval officers. "At last we've caught up with you and your thieving pirates, Johnny Poison!" the English captain cries, his pistol poised, aimed at the pirate's heart.

"Boy, are we glad to see you!" you cry, stepping forward.

"Get back, you sniveling snake!" the English captain yells, moving his pistol toward you. "Any more of your sarcastic talk, and we'll see that justice is done right here in these woods."

Go on to PAGE 39.

"You're making a big mistake," Mike says, unable to keep his voice from cracking.

"*You'll* be the one making the mistake if you take one step further," the captain says sternly.

"But we're not pirates!" you cry.

"And I'm a panda bear from Chinee!" The English captain laughs.

"This has *got* to be a dream!" you say to Mike. "This *can't* be happening! We'll open our eyes and be back in the museum. Right?"

Wrong.

There's only one cheerful note here: The British system of justice is recognized as the best in the world. Chances are you'll get off with a very light prison term of twenty or thirty years.

What's that? You'd rather close the book and take your chances on a different adventure?

You don't know when you're well off, do you?

THE END

"Let's go!" you yell. You start to run across the beach as fast as you can, heading for the woods.

It's hard to run on sand, and the angry pirates are right behind you. Suddenly, Mike slips and falls headfirst in front of you. You're running too fast to stop, and you trip over him and hit the sand.

"Get up—quick!" you cry, scrambling to your feet. "We can lose them if we get to the woods!"

"You're a dead one!" the pirate with the dagger yells. He's right behind you now. He's going to catch up. He's raising his dagger above his head.

Can you escape?

Turn to PAGE 52 to find out.

You raise the pistols and fire. The fight is a short one. The pirates do not expect you to have guns. You hit one, then another. They flee into the woods.

Ol' Jack is hopping up and down for joy. "Attaway, me lads! Attaway! I've got what they want! I've got what they want! Ha ha ha! An' Ol' Jack is holdin' on to it! Thank ye, me boys!"

"Let's see it! Open the chest!" you cry happily. "Mike, we're rich! We're—"

Ol' Jack takes out a rusted key and opens the treasure chest. He lifts the lid, and you see what is in the chest.

"I've got what they want! I've got what they want!" the old hermit sings. "But they ain't getting it! They ain't gettin' my coconuts!"

THE END

"Step lively, mates," calls the old pirate, leaning down over the bow of his ship, reaching a big hand toward you as you stare in amazement. "You don't want to make Captain Johnny angry now, do ye?"

"I don't know what's going on here—and I don't want to find out!" you cry. You and Mike turn and run without saying another word to each other.

"Ye'll regret this, ya swabs!" Captain Johnny yells, shaking his fists at you.

You start to run, but suddenly the floor seems to give way. There is a splash. All goes dark. You are in water now. You are swimming—swimming for your lives. Freezing waves wash against you as you struggle to keep afloat.

Cannons boom and a cannonball sails over your heads, exploding a few yards ahead of you in the water. You sputter and struggle against the waves. Turning back for a second, you see the pirate ship pursuing you at full sail.

The museum walls have disappeared, replaced by bright blue sky. The ocean is cold and dark around you as you and Mike swim, splashing and choking, with the ship right behind you.

"I don't believe it!" you try to yell to Mike, but your mouth fills with water. You decide to keep your mouth shut and swim!

Go on to PAGE 43.

"Look—over there!" Mike is pointing to your right.

Another cannonball sails over your heads and explodes, churning the water, sending up a giant wave that pushes you back toward Captain Johnny's ship.

"There's another ship over there!" Mike calls, pointing.

"And there's an island straight ahead," you cry.

"I can't tell whether the ship is another pirate ship or not!" Mike calls.

"Maybe we should head for the island," you say, bobbing above the harsh waves.

You must decide quickly. Captain Johnny Poison is closing in. Do you swim for the other ship—or the island?

If you choose to swim to the other ship, turn to PAGE 50.

If you choose to try your luck on the island, turn to PAGE 28.

Crash!

The skeletons shatter a giant glass display case as they rumble toward you.

"I don't understand how they can roar like that," Mike says, picking up a spear and a club from a display of ancient weapons. "They have no vocal cords or anything!"

"*That's* what you don't understand!" you cry. "How about the fact that these ancient piles of bones are walking around in here and seem to be on their way to eating us up alive? Do you understand that?!"

That's all the time for discussion that you two have. The prehistoric bears rise up on their hind legbones and prepare to attack.

"Spears? What good are spears against these monsters?" Mike cries. "We need machine guns!"

"Where are we going to find machine guns in the fossils room?" you cry.

Roooooaaaaaar!

The skeletons are circling the two of you now.

"Thank goodness there are only two of them," you say. You know it doesn't make any sense, but you're too frightened to make any sense.

"Yes, it's two against two—a fair fight," Mike says sarcastically.

Go on to PAGE 45.

The skeletons keep circling, not getting any closer, not going back any farther.

"I don't think they're going to attack," you tell Mike.

"Right. They're too afraid of us to attack," Mike says, still sarcastic.

Rooooaaaar!

You raise your spear and step forward to face them.

"Wait!" Mike cries. "Don't attack them!"

Should you wait and let them make the first move, or attack and maybe surprise them with your courage?

If you choose to wait till they make a move, turn to PAGE 54.

If you choose to attack first, turn to PAGE 62.

"I don't care *how* bright it is in there," Mike says. "The room has a curse on it. I can read. And I think we're in enough trouble without adding any ancient curses."

You have to agree that he's right this time.

"Okay, okay," you say reluctantly. "Let's try the dark doorway. But I know it's only going to lead to another dark room."

"Come on," Mike says, "don't you get discouraged. That's my job!"

You both laugh at his little joke. Then you step through the unmarked doorway.

You find yourself in an immense, dark room. Shining your flashlights all around, you see that the room is filled with large, long cases.

MUMMY CASES!

"Okay. You were right!" Mike cries. "The bright room! Let's go back and find the bright room. I'll take the curse. I'll take anything. Let's just get out of here!"

"They're only empty cases," you tell him, hoping that you are right. "Nothing to worry about. Look, there's another doorway up ahead. Let's keep walking and—"

You stop talking because you hear something.

What is that figure that is climbing out of the mummy case?

No. It can't be!

Can it?

Go on to PAGE 47.

You shine your flashlights onto the approaching figure.

Yes. It is. It's a mummy.

It's a mummy walking—with its arms outstretched toward you.

Turn to PAGE 72—and keep alert!

"Let him have his fun," you tell Mike. "We'll walk the plank and end up back in the museum room where we started."

"Get movin', the two of ye," Captain Johnny barks, pressing the tip of his sword in your back. "You two fakers will soon be endin' up as food for the fish."

"Right. We're going, we're going," you say, unable to hide your smile.

You and Mike confidently walk off the plank.

Splaaaaaaash!

Uh-oh. Things have not gone exactly as you planned. You are struggling to stay afloat, battling ocean waves. You swim away from the pirate ship, Captain Johnny's angry oaths fading from your ears.

"Where's the museum?" Mike asks. "Where are we?"

"Good questions," you reply, swallowing water as a wave spills over your head. "Hey—what's that up ahead?"

"It's another ship," Mike says. "It looks exactly like that replica of an old whaling ship—you know, the one in the next room."

You swim over to it. Sure enough, it's that very whaler. Sailors drop a line down to you and pull you up, wet and cold, from the sea. A sailor hands you blankets and sailor uniforms.

Go on to PAGE 49.

Suddenly you hear a voice cry out: "Whale on the starboard! Whale on the starboard!"

The entire ship swings into action. The harpoons are manned, nets are dropped.

"This is exciting," you say to Mike. "And look at these great uniforms."

"This scene is very familiar to me," Mike says, raising a harpoon as if to toss it at the whale. "It's just like the display in the museum."

"Put down that harpoon," you tell him, raising part of a giant net. "You're scaring me."

"I—I can't put it down," he replies, suddenly frightened. "I can't—move!"

"Here, I'll help," you say. But you can't move, either. You stand holding the net, staring out to sea, staring past Mike with his harpoon.

The next day the museum isn't very crowded. A few people come by the whaling ship display in the late afternoon. But no one notices the two new sailors who've been added to the display.

And no one—but you—realizes that this adventure in the Haunted Museum has come to an

END

Swimming hard, fighting the waves that choke and blind you, you head toward the large sailing ship to your right. The cannonballs burst all around you. The pirate ship is so close behind that you can hear Captain Johnny's angry oaths. But suddenly the pirate ship stops its pursuit. It turns and starts to sail in the other direction.

Exhausted, shaking from the cold and from your fear, you grab the line that is thrown to you from the ship you have struggled so hard to reach. As you are pulled up, you read the ship's name on the side: H.M.S. *Majestic*.

You and Mike have been pulled aboard a British naval ship! You eagerly grab the blankets that are handed to you.

"Glad you decided to abandon your captain," you hear a hearty English voice saying. "Perhaps you saw the error of your ways?"

"Well . . ." You're not sure what to say.

"Or perhaps you realized that we're about to blast Captain Johnny Poison out of the sea! That rascal has sailed his last *above* the ocean. We plan to send him sailing down *below* the ocean!"

"Sure. Okay," you mutter. You and Mike are relieved that you've escaped from the pirate captain—but *now* what have you gotten yourselves into?

Turn to PAGE 56 to find out.

The pirate slips and falls in the dry sand, and two of his cohorts topple over on top of him. While they scramble to get up, shoving each other and calling each other names, you and Mike reach the safety of the tangled woods.

"Stay low!" you yell, gasping for breath. The two of you duck down between the tall ferns and the bent, twisted palm trees.

The pirates have entered the woods. They are only a foot or two away from you, close enough to reach out and touch—but they don't see you. They walk right by, swearing loudly, kicking the ferns and underbrush out of their way.

You wait a minute or so and then quietly, carefully, begin walking in the other direction. Soon the woods give way to low hills. On the side of one of these hills, you and Mike find a cave. A small fire burns at the mouth of the cave.

"Someone lives here," you say.

"Yes, that be the truth," calls a voice from the darkness of the cave.

An old man with a long white beard down to his knees, dressed in rags that once were clothes, hobbles out of the cave. "Someone lives here—okay, okay. An' I be the one. I be livin' here for longer than ye've been walkin' this sad earth."

Go on to PAGE 53.

You start to say something to the old hermit, but he bursts into song, singing at the top of his lungs.

"Quiet, please!" you plead. "We're being followed by pirates, and we don't want—"

"Pirates? Hah! Ol' Jack has what they want! Ha ha ha! Come—look. I'll show you. I've got what those pirates want, but it's all mine! Mine!"

Ol' Jack leads you into his cave and shows you a large treasure chest, locked up tight. "I've got what they want!" He repeats it over and over.

Suddenly you hear a voice calling from outside the cave. "Come out of there, you two lubbers!"

You peer out and see that it's Captain Johnny Poison calling you. He and his men have joined the others in the hunt for you—and they've found you.

"I've got what they want!" Ol' Jack screams. "Help me! Don't let them take it— I'll split it with you!"

You must decide. Do you stay and fight off the pirates to get half of what's in the treasure chest? Or do you and Mike start running again and try to get to the pirate ship since the pirates are all on the island?

If you choose to stay and fight, turn to PAGE 61.

If you'd rather try to make it to the ship, turn to PAGE 81.

54

Roooaaaaar!

You back up. You keep backing up till you hit the wall. "What was I thinking of?" you yell.

"They're—they're closing in on us!" Mike screams.

You both press your backs against the far wall of the room and watch in horror as the two prehistoric beasts slowly approach.

"Help! Help!"

You find yourself screaming for help. Where is the night watchman? Where is somebody? Anybody?

The skeletons rise up again on their hind legs. Closer, closer they lurch, their ancient bones creaking as they walk.

Rooaaaar!

"Help! Somebody! Please—HELP!" You and Mike are both screaming now. You raise your spears and wait for the giant jaws to lower onto you.

Up, up, up reaches one of the skeleton bears and suddenly brings down its bony arm in a ferocious swipe—not at you, but at *the other skeleton!*

The other skeleton retaliates by clamping its toothy jaw onto the legbone of its companion. The two ancient bears are slashing at each other now, roaring, grunting, biting.

Go on to PAGE 55.

You and Mike watch in astonishment, still pressed against the wall. The two ancient bears are fighting each other, a battle to the death—except that they have been dead for thousands of years.

Another ferocious swipe, another, another. The room shakes and spins as the two combatants go at it with all the power of living monsters.

A few minutes later, the fight is over. The floor is strewn with giant bones. The skeletons have destroyed each other.

"Wow, that was—" You don't get to finish your sentence.

The lights go on. Two night watchmen burst into the room.

"What's going on here?" one of them shouts angrily.

They see the pile of bones, the skeletons in disarray all over the floor. "Oh, no! No!" one of them cries in horror.

"Uh . . . sir . . ." you begin. "Uh . . . we—we didn't do it!"

What do you think the chances are that you can make him believe you???

THE END

The H.M.S. *Majestic* picks up a strong gust of wind that carries it quickly toward the retreating pirate ship. The naval guns are poised and ready.

"What are we going to do?" Mike cries, timidly peering over the bow.

"What *can* we do?" you reply. "We're trapped—trapped in this sea battle. If we win, I guess . . ." You realize that you don't know *what* will happen to you if you win. And you don't want to think about what might happen to you should Captain Johnny Poison be victorious.

"Help us out if need be," the English captain says to you, his eyes straight ahead on the pirate ship, "and we'll see that things go easy for the two of you. I'll see that you only get prison terms when we get back to Portsmouth. You won't hang like the rest of those pirate dogs!"

Prison terms???

Does the English captain really think that you and Mike are pirates?

Of course he does. How else would you have been swimming away from a pirate ship?

You decide to try to explain to him what has happened to you—but the boom of cannons drowns out your frightened voice.

The battle is on.

Go on to PAGE 57.

Captain Johnny's cannons strike first, surprising the English captain. "Man the guns!" he screams, distressed that he was caught off guard.

The sky fills with smoke as the cannons from both ships send off a deafening roar.

"*Yaaaaiiiii!*" A sailor falls. Then another. Captain Johnny's guns are accurate—and deadly. Now the brig is on fire. The flames are spreading rapidly over the wooden ship.

"After them, men!" the English captain cries. Suddenly he grabs his chest. He crumples to the ground, victim of a bullet.

The sailors continue to fire despite the flames and despite the loss of their leader. But it is clear to everyone that Captain Johnny Poison is winning this battle.

"Give us a hand," a sailor calls. "We need your help to beat this pirate!"

Should you help? Should you man a cannon against Johnny Poison? If you do, the best that awaits you is a prison term.

Or should you just stand back and allow Johnny Poison to win? If he does, then what will happen to you?

If you choose to help, turn to PAGE 64.
If you choose to stay out of it, turn to PAGE 75.

As the mummy comes nearer, it seems to get taller. You soon begin to realize that this mummy is *over eight feet tall!*

An aroma of ancient decay fills your nostrils. You stagger back from the smell. You drop the bricks. You realize that trying to fight this monstrosity from the past would be futile.

"E-e-e-e-e-e-e!"

A high-pitched whistle pours out of the gaping hole that forms the mummy's mouth. The smell of decay is overpowering now. You feel as if you cannot breathe.

The ancient being lopes forward, stumbling and staggering, but always moving slowly, steadily, toward you and Mike. The decayed cloth falls from its body as it walks, leaving a gray trail of bandages on the dusty floor.

"E-e-e-e-e-e!"

The cry is mournful, tired, filled with the evil of centuries.

"Quick, Mike," you say, grabbing your friend. You realize that the two of you have been standing as if hypnotized, staring as the mummy approached. "Out that door over there. Run!"

But Mike stands there with his eyes wide and his mouth slightly open. He appears to be in a trance.

Go on to PAGE 59.

"Mike! Mike!" you scream as loudly as you can.

He doesn't seem to hear you.

You pull at him. "Come on, Mike—run!"

You can't pull him away. He is in the grip of the mummy's spell.

The mummy is close enough to grab you.

Do you try to pull Mike away, knowing that you probably aren't strong enough to escape while dragging him with you? Or do you leave Mike, run out as fast as you can, and hope you can find help in the museum?

If you choose to try to drag Mike away with you, turn to PAGE 69.

If you choose to run, turn to PAGE 78.

"These aren't ordinary owls!" you cry. "For one thing, they're three times as big as any owls I've ever seen!"

"And three times as mean!" Mike yells.

Without saying another word, the two of you run back through the door, back into the dark corridor from which you came.

The flapping wings are still crackling in your ears as you run, but the sound grows fainter and fainter.

The owls do not follow you out of the treasure room.

But now you are back in the twisting, curving corridors of this ancient pyramid. Unfortunately, you dropped your flashlights when you turned to run from the owls.

Deeper into the dark maze of halls you walk.

Will you find your way out?

Turn to PAGE 80.

"Help me, and I'll share my treasure," Ol' Jack says, his tired eyes pleading with you. He pulls out swords and pistols from the back of the cave. "All loaded and ready to go to work," he says, eagerly pushing the pistols into your hands.

You and Mike timidly creep up to the mouth of the cave. The pirates are pacing back and forth at the bottom of the hill. "Well . . . it's worth a try," you tell Mike.

You raise the pistol and prepare to fire.

Can you defeat the pirates and gain a share of Ol' Jack's treasure?

It's all a matter of luck.

If you're reading this book on a Monday, Wednesday, Friday, or Sunday, turn to PAGE 41.

If you're reading this book on a Tuesday, Thursday, or Saturday, turn to PAGE 93.

You thrust your spear up at the attacking skeleton. The room reverberates from the *claaaang* as ancient metal hits ancient bone. The beast is startled. It backs up a step, then another.

You thrust the spear forward again. Another *claaang*.

You look over to see how Mike is doing.

He raises his spear to defend himself from the slashing jaw of the other skeleton. But the ancient bear tosses Mike's spear away with one powerful swipe of his paw bones.

"Oh, no! I have no weapon!" Mike cries.

The skeleton rumbles in for the kill.

Can you save your friend? Is this the end for both of you?

Quick — turn to PAGE 76.

You strike the match against the match-book. Your hand trembles so much you can barely strike it. Finally the match flickers and then bursts into flame.

The skeletons seem to cry out. They back up, away from the flame. Back, back, they stagger. They have returned to their display cases. All is still again.

Suddenly the door bursts open behind you. The lights come on.

Into the room rushes the night watch-man, followed by your parents. "What are you doing here? Where have you been? We were so worried!" They rush forward with a steady stream of questions.

"What's been going on here?" the night watchman asks sternly.

"Oh, not much, really," you say, looking over at Mike. "It's been pretty quiet, actually." You pretend to yawn. "Very boring, I'm afraid."

"Well, don't you ever pull a stunt like this again!" your mother scolds.

She doesn't have to worry.

You'll never pull a stunt like this again—will you?

At least, not until the next time you open this book!

THE END

You and Mike rush forward to man the cannons, and the noisy battle continues. Now your guns begin to cause real damage, blasting big holes in the pirate ship. Screams of the wounded pirates compete with the explosions of the giant guns.

You learn quickly how to operate these powerful weapons—but still you may be too late! The entire deck of your ship is ablaze. You don't know how much longer you can stay aboard.

Suddenly the pirate ship bursts into flame. Fire consumes the ship in seconds. It founders and begins to sink.

"Farewell, farewell to Captain Johnny Poison!" a sailor sings out, watching the pirates fall into the sea as their ship sinks beyond view.

But it's also farewell to the H.M.S. *Majestic*, which is now beginning to sink. Suddenly the ship tilts forward without warning. You and Mike are thrown overboard, clear of the sinking ship, into the foaming, dark, ocean waters.

"Swim! Swim to the island!" you call to Mike.

Luckily, the tide is with you this time. It practically carries you to the sandy, deserted island you saw earlier. You both crawl onto the beach and turn to look for other survivors.

Go on to PAGE 65.

After a few minutes of watching the tumbling waves, you realize there *are* no other survivors.

"Hey—look! What's that?" Mike calls. He's pointing to something that has just drifted to shore from one of the ships. "It's a chest—a treasure chest!"

"Now, don't get all excited," you tell him, running over to open it as fast as you can. "It's probably just—"

GOLD!

An entire treasure chest of gold doubloons! You pick one up. It seems to weigh a ton.

"We're rich!" you are about to say.

But there is a blinding flash of light. You close your eyes. And when you open them, you find yourself back in the Caribbean Pirates Room of the museum.

The model of the pirate ship is standing right where it always has, with the pirate captain mannequin still on board. And in your hand is the gold doubloon—except that it no longer seems to weigh a ton, since it is made of gold tinfoil.

"I don't believe it," you say wearily to Mike. "I guess none of it really happened, none of it."

But if that is true . . . why are you both dripping wet?!?

THE END

The mummy stops. It seems to be looking all around the room, even though its ancient eyes are covered with tar and decayed cloth.

"It stopped!" Mike cries.

"I can see!" you say. "Do you think the bricks are giving him second thoughts?"

The mummy starts toward you again.

"No, I guess it wasn't the bricks," you say, a sinking feeling starting in the pit of your stomach and working its way up.

"E-e-e-e-e-e!"

The mummy seems to be laughing at you, hideous laughter through decayed lips.

You drop the two bricks.

"I must've been crazy to think I could fight this creature with bricks!" you cry.

You and Mike have backed up as far as you can.

Still the mummy lumbers forward, pieces of its body falling off as it moves deliberately toward you.

"A match!" you cry, getting an idea. "Do we have any matches? We'll burn him! We'll set him on fire!"

"There's only one problem with that idea," Mike says quietly.

"What's that?"

"We don't have any matches."

"E-e-e-e-e-e!"

Go on to PAGE 67.

The mummy seems to be enjoying your terror.

Closer, closer it comes, reaching out, reaching for you, reaching to envelop you in the stench of its moldy wrappings.

Your backs against the wall, you could not run now even if you chose to.

You both make fists. You prepare for a fight. You prepare for what will probably be the final fight of your lives.

Or will it?

Turn to PAGE 70.

"There must be millions and millions of dollars worth of treasure here," you tell Mike, pulling him away from the exit. "We can't just leave it, we can't!"

Mike thinks about it for a moment. "I guess you're right," he says finally. "I guess it's worth a try, anyway. But you're forgetting about the curse, aren't you?"

"Of course I'm forgetting about the curse," you tell him. "I don't believe in junk like that. Now, come on — help me drag this chest out of here."

Soon you both realize that it isn't going to be easy to move the chest, even the short distance to the exit. It's really heavy, and it feels as if it's been resting against that wall for thousands of years.

Finally, with you pulling and Mike pushing as hard as you can, you begin to slide it slowly across the dusty floor of the treasure chamber.

"It's moving! It's moving! We're gonna do it!" you cry.

Will you get the chest safely out through the exit?

Turn to PAGE 88.

You grab Mike by both shoulders and pull.

He seems to be rooted to the floor. You're using all your strength, but you can't budge him.

"Mike! Mike!" you scream right in his ear. But he doesn't give any sign at all of hearing you.

"E-e-e-e-e!"

The whistle sounds like laughter now.

The mummy is only two feet away. Its arms are close enough to reach you.

The smell. The smell is overwhelming you. You feel faint.

You realize you must forget about Mike. You must try to save yourself.

Quick. Let go of him.

Run. Run for your life.

And turn to PAGE 86.

"E-e-e-e-e-e!"

The mummy raises its ancient head, and the eerie laughter whistles through its throat.

"Well," you say to Mike, "we wanted to find out if the rumors about this museum are true or not. I guess we found out!"

"That cheers me up a lot," Mike says sarcastically.

The mummy has stopped once again.

Perhaps he is savoring his victory. Perhaps he is deciding whether to handle one of you at a time or both of you at once.

You pick up the bricks again.

Without stopping to think, you throw them at the mummy with all your strength.

The bricks go right *through* him!

He stretches a huge, tarred hand out to grab you.

His hand goes right through you!

He grabs at you again. And again.

You feel nothing. He is in another dimension. He cannot reach you. He is harmless.

He begins to stagger forward.

He walks right through you. You don't feel a thing. He walks through the stone wall. He disappears.

Still shaking, you turn to Mike. "He . . . he's a . . . ghost . . . or something!"

Go on to PAGE 71.

A few minutes later, you and Mike have regained enough composure to go back into the dark corridors of the pyramid. Soon you find the exit.

You step out into the familiar museum room. Light pours in from the window— it's morning. "Look, Mike!" you cry. "The night watchman!"

You go running over to him.

"Hey, what are you two rascals doing here?" he cries angrily. "If you've been up to no good, I'll—"

"It was the mummy!" you blurt out. "The mummy! He came to life! He chased us! Really! We're not putting you on! Look at us! Look how scared we are! You've got to believe us! The mummy—it chased us!" The words all tumble out.

The night watchman squints at you. "I'm sorry, kid. You'll have to do better than that."

"But the mummy—"

"We don't have a mummy in this museum," the night watchman says sternly. "We haven't had a mummy for months. We had to send it back to Cairo for repairs."

You turn back to show him where the mummy chased you inside the pyramid. But in the light of day, you see that the pyramid is only four feet tall — not even big enough for two people to squeeze inside at once!

THE END

"Wh-what do you th-think he wants?" Mike asks, so terrified he can barely talk.

You're just as terrified as Mike. "I—I don't care what he wants," you manage to say. You bend down and pick up two bricks off the floor. "This should discourage him from coming any closer!"

"You—you're going to fight him?!" Mike cries. "Let's just get out of here!"

"Look how slow he is," you say, trying to give yourself confidence. "He's old, right? We can take him, Mike!"

You raise the bricks and prepare to throw them as the mummy staggers closer, closer, closer.

You must choose quickly—run or fight?

If you choose to run from the approaching mummy, turn to PAGE 58.

If you choose to stay and fight him off, turn to PAGE 66.

74

Keep walking.

Don't stop.

It isn't possible that you are going around in circles—and that you will be going around in circles forever.

Is it???

Turn to PAGE 80.

"Get back, Mike," you call to your friend. "Quick—hide over here. The fire is getting closer!"

The two of you duck behind a mast.

A few minutes later, the battle is lost. The H.M.S. *Majestic* is covered in flames—her sailors wounded, dying, or about to abandon ship.

Captain Johnny's laughter can be heard over the *crack-crack-crack* of the few pistols still being fired. The pirate ship pulls alongside the doomed naval ship.

The bow of the *Majestic* tilts up in the air. The ship starts to sink. Moments later, you and Mike are bobbing in the water, holding on desperately to planks from the ship. Captain Johnny stands above you with a wide smile across his powder-blackened face.

"Help us! Please! Pull us out!" you call up to him.

"I'd like to," Captain Johnny calls down. "But I can't, don't you know. I'm a *bad* guy — remember?"

Then he sails away.

A punch line like that could dampen your spirits, couldn't it? You probably agree that this ending is all wet! Well . . . take deep breaths and keep paddling, or close the book and then dive back into a different adventure!

THE END

"Where's my spear? I can't find it! It's so dark in here!" Mike screams.

You get an idea.

You reach into your pocket and search around until you find what you're looking for — a book of matches.

"I'll light a match so you can see!" you cry. Will there be time to retrieve the spear and fend off the attacking bear skeletons?

There *has* to be!

You light a match. "There it is, Mike!" you yell, pointing to the spear on the dark floor a few yards away.

But wait. What's going on?

The room is silent. The bears have stopped their pursuit. They are standing still, up on their hind legs, creaking, quivering.

You light another match.

They arch back in fright.

You take a step forward, holding the match up high in front of you.

They step back. Then they take a few more steps back.

"They're afraid!" you cry to Mike. "It's fire! They're afraid of fire."

You light another match. They back up. They are almost back to their display cases. Do you have enough matches to hold them off?

Go on to PAGE 77.

You look down and see that you have only one more match. You have no choice but to light it.

Can you defeat these ghostly skeletons with this one remaining match?

Turn to PAGE 63 to find out.

"Mike! Mike!" you are screaming right in his ear, but he doesn't hear you. He doesn't move.

You realize you must run. You cannot save him.

But where can you run? Back into the dark corridors?

If only you could find an exit, find your way back to the museum, perhaps you could get the night watchman. Then you could bring him into the pyramid and the two of you could rescue Mike.

"I'll be back, Mike!" you yell, praying that he can hear you. "I'm not deserting you! I'll be back! I promise!"

You turn and run.

Just before you reach the door, you look back. The mummy is right in front of Mike, reaching for Mike, grabbing Mike. And Mike stands still and silent, staring at the wall and seeing nothing.

You run out into the dark corridor.

You trip over something.

You pick it up. It's a long stick with a metal point attached on one end.

A spear!

Perhaps it isn't too late. Perhaps you can rescue Mike after all.

Go on to PAGE 79.

What good would a spear be against the ancient magic the mummy possesses?

Suddenly, through the next doorway, you see some familiar things. It is the museum room. You've found the exit!

Perhaps the night watchman is nearby. Now you must make a choice.

Should you take the spear, return to face the mummy, and rescue your friend? Or should you leave the pyramid, go into the museum, and find the night watchman to help you rescue Mike?

If you choose to try your luck with the spear, turn to PAGE 87.

If you choose to try to find the night watchman, turn to PAGE 84.

80

"I know we've been here before," Mike says.

"How can you tell?" you ask. "It's so dark, we can't even see if there are footprints in the dust."

You both stop for a moment.

"We'll just keep walking straight. And we'll only make left turns."

"Good idea," Mike says, but you can tell from his voice that he doesn't think it will work.

"Come on. We can't stop. I know the exit must be straight ahead."

Is the exit straight ahead? Turn to PAGE 89.

"Sorry, Ol' Jack," you tell the hermit, "but we're no match for an entire band of pirates. We've got to try and escape."

"I'll help you," Ol' Jack says. "Just flap your arms real hard and fly up in the trees the way I do sometimes."

"No. I think we'll stay on the ground," you say. And you and Mike run out of the cave and down the hill, heading toward the woods with the pirates in fast pursuit.

Once again you manage to lose them in the woods. Soon you find yourselves back on the sandy beach. "Look—Captain Johnny's canoe!" you cry. "What luck!"

In seconds, the two of you are in the canoe, rowing out to the pirate ship. "If we can lift anchor," you tell Mike, "the pirates will be stranded on the island, and we can try to sail for land."

But as soon as you get aboard the pirate ship, you see another ship drawing near. "Look—it's a British naval ship!" Mike cries. "Help us! Help! We're here!" he calls.

They reply with gunfire. Soon cannon-balls are bombarding your ship. What a shame! They must think you're pirates! But you really can't blame them, can you?

Ever get that *sinking feeling* that you're in big trouble? Do you begin to get the idea that, since this page ends with *GLUB GLUB GLUB*, this might just be

THE END

"Look, Mike— I *knew* this was the right room!" you cry, pointing to a doorway you hadn't noticed before. "There's an exit sign over that door—a modern exit sign just like all the others in the museum!"

"Whooppeee!!" Mike cries. "Let's go!"

"But what about the treasure?" you ask. "Look at all these old coins and all these jewels? We'll be rich, Mike! We can't just leave this stuff here."

"Oh, yes, we can!" Mike cries, heading toward the exit sign.

You must make a big decision here.

Should you leave the treasure in this room and get out of the pyramid as fast as you can? Or should you drag the treasure chest out with you?

If you choose to leave without the treasure, turn to PAGE 90.

If you'd rather drag the treasure out with you, turn to PAGE 68.

The night watchman probably carries a gun!

But what good would a gun be against an immortal mummy from ancient Egypt?

Well, it would certainly be better than a stupid spear.

These are the thoughts that rush through your mind as you run toward the doorway that seems to lead back to the museum.

You have other thoughts, too:

What if the night watchman doesn't believe my story? Who would believe my story? What if he thinks I'm just another kid playing another prank on him?

You run and run, but the doorway doesn't seem to be getting any closer. Is it some sort of optical illusion? Are you actually running toward nothing at all?

"E-e-e-e-e-e!"

Another mummy pops its decaying head out from a side corridor.

You scream. It makes a grab for you and misses. You keep running. Terror drives you now; terror makes you run faster than you've ever run before.

"E-e-e-e-e-e!"

Another hideous whistle from another hideous mummy. This one attempts to block your path.

You run right into it. You can't stop yourself.

Go on to PAGE 85.

It topples over backward, gives another eerie whistle, then disappears.

You keep running. You are almost to the door now. You can see the museum room on the other side.

It's morning, and the room is bright.

Just a few more steps now.

You're going to make it. You're almost there.

You're THERE!

You're out of the pyramid! You're back in the museum!

And there, standing in front of you, you see him—the night watchman!

"Help!" you scream, gasping, choking for air. "Please—help!"

He hears you. He turns around. He tilts back his night watchman's cap. He—

HE'S A MUMMY, TOO!!!

What did you expect in the Haunted Museum?

A happy ending?!?

THE END

You can stop trying to run.

It won't do you any good.

You realize that now, don't you?

Once Mike was under the mummy's spell, you realized it wouldn't be long before you were captured by it, as well.

The mummy's magic is pretty powerful. But of course he's had several thousand years to perfect it.

Perhaps you will have that long to perfect your magic.

Yes, yes. The mummifying process was a bit painful, wasn't it? You don't exactly feel like yourself anymore.

You both don't *look* like yourselves anymore, either.

It's lucky that you look so good in gray gauze!

Here's a thought to cheer you up. Sometime soon, some other kids are going to get the crazy idea to spend a night in the museum. And somehow they will certainly find themselves wandering through the chambers of the ancient pyramid.

And when that happens . . . *you'll* be ready for them.

Won't you?

THE END

You hold the spear high and run back to the room where the mummy pursued you. "Prepare for a fight!" you scream, hoping to startle the mummy.

But the room has disappeared.

You find yourself outdoors. The bright sun forces you to shield your eyes.

When you can see properly, you realize you are in a crowded city. Hundreds of workers are walking in a line. Each is carrying a brick. They are building . . .

A PYRAMID!

Is it possible? Have you walked back in time, back to ancient Egypt?

But where is the mummy? And where is Mike?

Turn to PAGE 92 for some of the answers.

"We did it! We're out!"

With your last burst of strength you push the large treasure chest out through the exit. You look around. You are standing in the Ancient Egyptian Room of the museum.

You can see through the window that the sun is starting to come up. It's almost morning. You've been inside that pyramid all night!

"Open the chest!" Mike cries. "Let's take a good look at our millions!"

Together you lift open the heavy top of the treasure chest and stare inside.

The chest is filled with dust.

The treasure has all turned to dust. You have just discovered the curse of the ancient treasure. It cannot be removed from its resting place!

"There goes our fortune," Mike says wearily. "Come on, let's call home. One of our parents can come pick us up. I want to go home."

You both search through your pockets. Neither one of you has a dime.

The only way you can get out of the museum is to close the book. And you might as well, since this surely is

THE END

"Keep going, keep going," you urge Mike. "I know we're going the right way. I just know it."

"Maybe this is the curse," Mike says, even gloomier. "We'll be walking through these halls forever."

"You've seen too many movies," you say. "Keep walking. Here. Turn left. And another left turn."

You're both walking very slowly now. You're thinking about the curse and about how each room you come to looks exactly like all the others.

But don't give up hope. Keep walking and turn left to PAGE 74.

"I'm getting out of here!" Mike cries. "I don't care about the treasure! I just want out!" He runs toward the door.

You agree that he is right, and you quickly follow him. The two of you burst through the exit door, out of the old pyramid, and into the familiar museum room.

"Hey, you two—what are you doing here?"

It's the night watchman. You've run right out in front of him.

"Man, are we glad to see you!" you cry. "We've been trapped in this pyramid all night."

"That's right," Mike says. "We've been wandering from room to room, down one hall and then another. We couldn't find our way out!"

The night watchman looks at you both as if you're crazy. "You two are going to have to come up with a better story than that!" he says, laughing at you.

"It's true! It's true!" you both insist.

The night watchman laughs again. "It can't be true," he says. "That pyramid isn't real or anything. It's a hollow shell. It's just a stage prop some movie company gave us!"

"What do you mean?" you ask. "That can't be! We—"

"Come, I'll show you," he says, leading you back to the door you just came out of.

Go on to PAGE 91.

He opens the door and you look inside.
The pyramid is indeed a hollow shell.
No corridors. No rooms. No halls. No owls.
No treasure room or treasure.

The night watchman closes the door and
leads you to his small office. "Now, suppose
you tell me what *really* happened to you
tonight."

"Uh . . . you go first," Mike says.

Go ahead. Tell him!

THE END

92

"Spear carrier!" a stern voice calls. "Spear carrier! Can you not hear me?"

A tall man in a military helmet is speaking. After a while, you realize he is speaking to *you!*

"Spear carrier, hurry the line! It is too slow!" he orders.

You look down and realize that you are still carrying the spear. You rush forward to do as you have been ordered.

"Hurry the line!" you call to the workers, who unhappily begin to move forward with their bricks as you brandish the spear.

Looking over the line of slaves, you suddenly see a familiar face.

"Mike!" you cry in astonishment, dropping the spear in surprise.

Mike looks up for a brief second. He is struggling under the weight of a large brick. He looks away. The line moves forward.

You pick up the spear. "Hurry the line, slaves!" you yell. You can't worry about Mike or about anything else.

You've got a job to do.

And you know that if you don't do it well, it will be

THE END

You raise the pistol and pull the trigger. Nothing happens.

You try another pistol. Nothing. You look inside one of the pistols. It's filled with sand.

"Hey, Ol' Jack," you call. "These pistols are all filled with sand."

"Don't ye think I know it?" Ol' Jack says. "That's all I could find here in this cave. And take a look at this!" He flings open the top of the treasure chest. The chest is filled to the top with sand.

You are too disappointed to speak. You turn back toward the pirates and discover that they have climbed the hill and are now at the mouth of the cave. "Now we've got ye!" one of them yells. He rushes forward and begins shaking you by the shoulder.

He's shaking your shoulder, shaking you . . . shaking you . . .

Suddenly you realize it isn't a pirate at all. It's the museum night watchman who is shaking you. "Are you okay?" he asks in a worried voice. "You took a nasty fall off that pirate ship. You've been unconscious for nearly ten minutes!"

Is it possible? It was all just a crazy dream?

You look around. "What is all this sand doing on the floor?" you ask.

The night watchman has no answer!

THE END